All My Kisses

Kerry Brown

Illustrated by Jedda Robaard

ABC
Books

The ABC 'Wave' device and the 'ABC KIDS' device are trademarks of the Australian Broadcasting Corporation and are used under licence by HarperCollins*Publishers* Australia.

First published in Australia in 2014
This paperback edition published in 2015
by HarperCollins*Children'sBooks*
a division of HarperCollins*Publishers* Australia Pty Limited
ABN 36 009 913 517
harpercollins.com.au

Text copyright © Kerry Brown 2014
Illustrations copyright © Jedda Robaard 2014

The rights of Kerry Brown and Jedda Robaard to be identified as the author and illustrator of this work have been asserted by them in accordance with the *Copyright Amendment (Moral Rights) Act 2000*.

HarperCollins*Publishers*
Level 13, 201 Elizabeth Street, Sydney, NSW 2000, Australia
Unit D1, 63 Apollo Drive, Rosedale, Auckland 0632, New Zealand
A 53, Sector 57, Noida, UP, India
1 London Bridge Street, London SE1 9GF, United Kingdom
2 Bloor Street East, 20th floor, Toronto, Ontario M4W 1A8, Canada
195 Broadway, New York NY 10007, USA

National Library of Australia Cataloguing-in-Publication entry

Brown, Kerry, 1972 – author.
    All my kisses / written by Kerry Brown, illustrated by Jedda Robaard.
    ISBN: 978 0 7333 3071 1 (hardback)
    ISBN: 978 0 7333 3272 2 (paperback)
    For preschool age.
    Sharing—Juvenile fiction.
    Kissing—Juvenile fiction.
A823.4

Designed by Jane Waterhouse
Cover illustration by Jedda Robaard
Colour reproduction by Graphic Print Group, Adelaide
Printed and bound in China by RR Donnelley on 128gsm Matt Art

7 6 5   17 18 19

For Kiv – STILL.
Thanks to Helen and Madeline
for igniting the spark.
KB

For my three favourite
little piggies, with love.
JR

Abby was very **kissable**.

Each night as she snuggled into bed,
she would be **kissed.**

Once on the end of her nose,

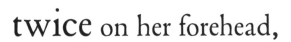

twice on her forehead,

and **countless** times all
over the bottom of her feet.

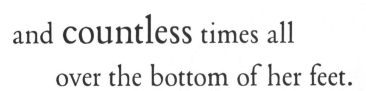

Abby **loved** her kisses.

She collected each one and
kept them in a special bucket.

Abby carried her kisses everywhere
and she **never let them go.**

Even if someone **asked** for one ...

or **needed** one!

'Would you like to pass your kisses around?' her teacher asked during Show and Tell one day.

'No!' said Abby, tucking them
safely under her arm.

'My kisses are too special.'

'Can I hold your kisses so that
you can swim?' Daddy offered.

'No!' said Abby.

'My kisses are too precious!'

'Why don't you send a kiss to Grandma Nellie
for her birthday?' Mummy suggested.

'No!' said Abby.
'My kisses are too fragile!'

Abby's kisses continued to grow and grow and grow, until her bucket was almost overflowing.

Soon the kisses at the bottom of the bucket could no longer be seen.

Slowly, these forgotten kisses began to lose their special glow.

Until one day, all that could be
found inside Abby's bucket was
a pile of **bleak, grey** pebbles.

Abby carried her bucket
outside and threw the pebbles
into the shadows.

That night, when Abby went to bed,
she felt **cold** and **lonely**.

The next day, Abby was
surprised to find that her pebbles were
no longer scattered across the ground.

Instead they were
in the **sandpit,**

on top of
sandcastles

and inside other children's buckets!

Laughter filled the air.

Abby watched as her small grey pebbles

were **tossed** ...

and **buried,**

and **shared** between friends.

As the afternoon sun began to fade and the children ran home for dinner, Abby noticed the pebbles starting to glow.

By nightfall, as if greeting the stars,
     the pebbles shone **bright** and **true.**

That evening, Abby's heart
felt **warm** and **light**.

She couldn't wait to collect
more kisses …

... and **share** them around.